Percy Pengelly
and the wibble-wobble

A story from Cornwall

Jenny Steele Scolding
Andy McPherson

Percy Pengelly worked in the circus. He was a tightrope walker. Every summer the circus came to Cornwall. This made Percy very happy because Cornwall was his home.

Percy was a tall, thin man with a long, droopy moustache. He wore a sparkly coat which twinkled in the circus lights. Every day when the band played, the ringmaster waited in the circus ring. Then the music stopped.

'Ssh,' said the children.

'Ssh,' said the mums and dads.

Everyone was quiet. Everyone waited.

Suddenly the trumpets blew – toot-toot-toot – toot-toot-toot – and Percy ran into the circus ring. His sparkly coat twinkled.

'Percy Pengelly!' shouted the ringmaster. 'The bravest man in Cornwall! The best tightrope walker in the world! The mag-ni-fi-cent, the spec-tac-u-lar, Percy Pengelly!'

Percy bowed, and everyone clapped and clapped.

Then Percy climbed a tall
ladder. Up, up, up he went until
he reached the tightrope which
stretched from pole to pole, high
above the circus ring.

Where the tightrope joined
each pole, there was a platform
and when Percy reached the
platform, the drums rolled –
de-dum-de-dum-de-dum – and
the cymbals crashed.

The children stopped shouting.

The mums and dads stopped talking.

Everyone looked up, up, up. Everyone looked up at Percy Pengelly. They knew that if he wibble-wobbled he might fall. It was dangerous to wibble-wobble. Very, very dangerous.

Percy picked up a long stick to help him balance. He didn't look down at the children far below. He didn't look down at the mums and dads. He held his head up high and with slow, careful steps he walked across the tightrope to the other side.

But Percy wasn't always so careful. Sometimes, half way across the rope, he did a little dance.

Wibble-wobble, wibble-wobble, wibble-wobble!

The children screamed. They didn't want him to fall. But Percy Pengelly had worked in the circus for years and years and he had never ever fallen off the tightrope.

Then one day Percy was afraid. He was getting old and he didn't like it when the tightrope went up and down beneath his feet. It only moved a teeny-weeny bit, but it made his heart go pitter-patter.

'I must be brave,' he said to himself, but when he stepped onto the tightrope he wibble-wobbled far too much. He wibble-wobbled more than ever before.

Wibble-wobble, wibble-wobble, wibble-wobble!

'Oh no!' screamed the children. 'He's going to fall.'

'He looks ill,' said the mums and dads. 'He looks wisht.'

Percy Pengelly didn't fall. He walked safely to the other side, but all the time he was afraid. His heart went pitter-patter and he felt sick.

The ringmaster had been watching the wibble-wobbles.

'Percy Pengelly!' he shouted. 'Too many wibble-wobbles! You nearly fell. You can't work in the circus any more.'

'Oh no!' said Percy. 'I can't leave the circus. I need a job. Give me one more chance, ringmaster. I'll try not to wibble-wobble too much.'

'No!' said the ringmaster. 'You have to go.'

Percy began to cry. Tears ran down his cheeks. The clowns did tricks to cheer him up, but he went on crying. He took off his sparkly coat and gave it back to the ringmaster.

'Goodbye, ringmaster,' he said. 'Goodbye, clowns.'

He walked sadly away from the circus.

Poor Percy! He needed a job.

Can you think of a job for Percy Pengelly?

First of all, Percy got a job in a fish shop. He didn't like it.

'It's a stinky, stinky job,' he said.

Then he got a job on a rubbish lorry. He hated emptying the bins.

'It's a stinky, stinky job,' he said.

After that he got a job at the zoo. He cleaned up the tiger poo. He cleaned up the penguin poo. He cleaned up the elephant poo. He cleaned up all the poo in the zoo.

'It is a stinky, stinky job,' he said. 'I want to go back to the circus.'

But Percy Pengelly couldn't work at the circus any more.

Why?

Because he wibble-wobbled too much.

Then one day he saw a van and printed on the side in big letters were the words: CHIMNEY SWEEP. Percy smiled a big, big smile. Percy laughed a big, big laugh.

Why do you think he was smiling? What was he going to do?

A few days later Percy went shopping. He bought a ladder and tied it onto the roof of his new van. He bought a sweep's brush to stick up chimneys, and a vacuum cleaner to suck up soot. He put them in the back of his van and drove away.

He parked his van by a row of houses near the sea. He untied the ladder. He took out the sweep's brush and the vacuum cleaner.

Then Percy knocked on the door of house number one. Rat-a-tat-tat. Mr Pascoe opened the door.

'Percy Pengelly, me 'ansome,' he said, 'where's your sparkly coat?'

'I've left the circus,' said Percy. 'I'm a chimney sweep now.'

'Good,' said Mr Pascoe. 'My chimney needs sweeping and I think it's blocked.'

Percy knocked on the door of house number two. Rat-a-tat-tat. Mrs Trewin opened the door.

'Percy Pengelly, my bird,' she said, 'where's your sparkly coat?'

'I've left the circus,' said Percy. 'I'm a chimney sweep now.'

'Good,' said Mrs Trewin. 'The chimney needs sweeping and my Jenna has lost her kite. See if it's up there on the roof, will 'ee?'

Percy knocked on the door of house number three. Rat-a-tat-tat. Mrs Roskilly opened the door.

'Percy Pengelly, my luvver,' she said, 'where's your sparkly coat?'

'I've left the circus,' said Percy. 'I'm a chimney sweep now.'

'Proper job,' said Mrs Roskilly. 'My chimney needs sweeping, too.'

Percy knocked on the door of house number four. Rat-a-tat-tat. Captain Lugg opened the door.

'Percy Pengelly,' said Captain Lugg. 'I've no time for chit-chat. I'm going fishing,' and he stanked off down the road to the harbour.

Percy Pengelly was happy. He had lots of work. He went inside each house and pushed his brush up the chimney. Down fell the dirty black soot. He sucked it up with his vacuum cleaner and then he went outside.

He put his ladder up against the wall of house number one and he climbed up, up, up, onto the top of the roof.

Mr Pascoe, Mrs Trewin and Mrs Roskilly all looked up at him.

'I hope he doesn't wibble-wobble,' said Mr Pascoe.

'I hope he doesn't wibble-wobble,' said Mrs Trewin.

'I hope he doesn't wibble-wobble,' said Mrs Roskilly.

'Be careful, Percy Pengelly!' they all shouted.

Percy Pengelly stood on the top of the roof. It was very high, but it didn't go up and down like the tightrope in the circus. It didn't move even a teeny-weeny bit. It was hard under his feet. He took a deep breath and walked across the rooftop to the first chimney.

And he didn't wibble-wobble. He didn't wibble-wobble at all.

When Percy looked inside Mr. Pascoe's chimney he saw a bird sitting on some sticks. It was a jackdaw and the sticks were its nest.

'Go away, jackdaw!' said Percy, 'Shoo! When Mr Pascoe lights his fire the smoke will come up the chimney and burn your bottom!'

The jackdaw flew away. Percy pulled all the sticks out of the chimney pot. He put a net over the top, so the birds couldn't build any more nests there. Then he walked along the rooftop to the next chimney.

And he didn't wibble-wobble. He didn't wibble-wobble at all.

When Percy Pengelly got to Mrs Trewin's chimney, can you guess what he found? It was the kite lost by her little girl, Jenna, and its tail was caught on the television aerial!

Percy was just untying the kite when he heard seagulls squawking. Their nest was on a ledge near the chimney and they didn't want Percy to go near their baby chicks. They flew at his face and tried to peck his nose.

Percy grabbed the kite, threw it down to Mrs Trewin, and then he ran away across the rooftop.

And he didn't wibble-wobble. He didn't wibble-wobble at all.

At last he got to Mrs Roskilly's roof. Oh dear, one of the bricks on the chimney was loose. He wiggled it and waggled it and pushed it in tight. Then he put a net over the top of the chimney pot. Do you remember why?

So the birds couldn't build any nests there!

Mr Pascoe, Mrs Trewin and Mrs Roskilly moved the ladder to the other end of the row of houses so that Percy could climb down. They waited and they waited but he didn't come.

'Where's he to?' said Mr Pascoe.

'Where's he to?' said Mrs Trewin.

'Where's he to?' said Mrs Roskilly.

'Where is Percy Pengelly?' they all shouted.

Percy was sitting on the roof with his back against a chimney pot. The sea was blue and the sun was warm on his face. He saw Captain Lugg's boat going up and down on the waves and the seagulls flying after the fishing boats.

'Cornwall is the most beautiful place in the world,' he said to himself.

Suddenly Percy saw that Captain Lugg was in trouble. He was leaning over the side of the boat trying to pull up his lobster pots, but the rope was tangled.

Then, splash! Captain Lugg fell into the sea. As he hit the water his lifejacket filled with air. It blew up like a balloon and Captain Lugg floated along on top of the water.

'Help!' he shouted, as the waves carried him away from his boat. 'Help! Help!'

Percy Pengelly took his phone out of his bag and phoned the coastguard. 'Quick!' he shouted. 'Send the lifeboat. Captain Lugg's fallen off his boat. He's in the sea!'

Percy whizzed down the roof on his bottom. Mr Pascoe, Mrs Trewin and Mrs Roskilly were all standing at the foot of the ladder.

'Captain Lugg's in the sea!' he told them. 'The lifeboat will be here dreckly.'

Percy climbed back up the roof. He leant against the chimney pot and he waited. He could see Captain Lugg far away, floating on the waves.

Then Percy saw the lifeboat. It was going very fast. Percy watched the strong lifeboat crew pull Captain Lugg out of the sea.

'The lifeboat's arrived!' shouted Percy Pengelly.

'Lifeboat's here!' shouted Mr Pascoe.

'Lifeboat's here!' shouted Mrs Trewin.

'Lifeboat's here!' shouted Mrs Roskilly.

'Hooray! Hooray!' they all shouted. 'The lifeboat's here!'

Percy Pengelly climbed down the ladder. Mr Pascoe, Mrs Trewin and Mrs Roskilly all patted him on the back.

'Well done,' they said, and 'Proper job!'

They paid him for cleaning the chimneys and were just having a cup of tea when they heard a car. The coastguards had arrived, and who do you think was with them?

It was Captain Lugg! He was warm and dry, safe and sound.

Percy Pengelly tied the ladder onto the roof of his van. He took the chimney sweep's brush and the vacuum cleaner and put them in the back. Then he drove home.

He ate a pasty for his supper. He drank a cup of tea. He stroked his cat, and he smiled and smiled. 'What a day!' he said to himself. 'I've done so many things.'

What had Percy done on his first day as a chimney sweep?

He'd chased away the jackdaw.

He'd cleared away the nest of sticks.

He'd put nets over the top of the chimney pots.

He'd run away from the angry seagulls.

He'd found Jenna's kite.

He'd wiggle-waggled the brick to make it tight.

And... he'd saved Captain Lugg.

'I like being a chimney sweep,' Percy told his cat. 'I like it very much. It's much more fun than being a tightrope walker... and do you know what?'

'I didn't wibble-wobble. I didn't wibble-wobble at all!'

THE END

Percy's Picture Quiz

Look closely at the pictures in this book and see if you can find:

3 cats, 3 kites and 3 jackdaws
1 robin and 4 fish
1 bicycle and 5 yellow vans

and how many seagulls
can you count?
There are more than 30!

CHIMNEY SWEEP

www. pengelly-soot-buster.co.uk